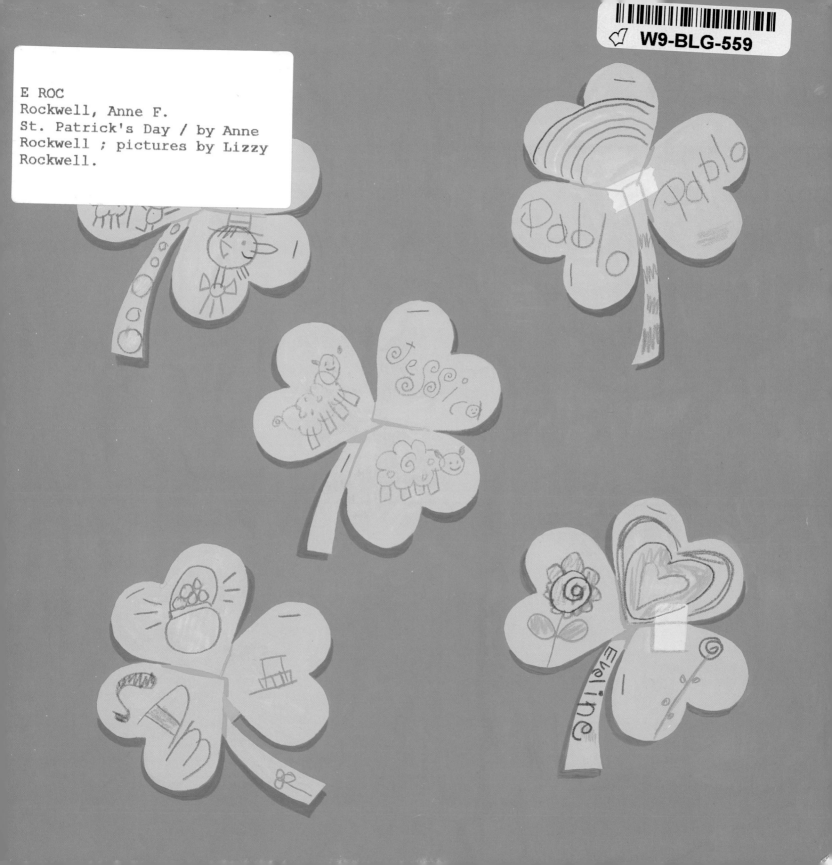

For our Irish neighbors, however far we roam,
Betty O'Brien Weihs and her Bill,
and their gang,
Bill, Tim, Chris, Jackie and Stacie
plus their gangs
Tyler, Evy, and Katherine,
Grant, Maddie and Cole,
Christopher and Caroline,
Megan, Peter, and Charlie
and Michael

St. Patrick's Day
Text copyright © 2010 by Anne Rockwell   Illustrations copyright © 2010 by Lizzy Rockwell
Manufactured in China. All rights reserved. No part of this book may be used or reproduced in
any manner whatsoever without written permission except in the case of brief quotations embodied
in critical articles and reviews. For information address HarperCollins Children's Books, a
division of HarperCollins Publishers, 10 East 53rd Street, New York, NY 10022.
www.harpercollinschildrens.com
Library of Congress Cataloging-in-Publication Data
Rockwell, Anne F. St. Patrick's Day / by Anne Rockwell ; pictures by Lizzy Rockwell. — 1st ed.   p. cm.
Summary: Mrs. Madoff's students celebrate Saint Patrick's Day by making class presentations
about the history of the holiday and Irish traditions and culture.   ISBN 978-0-06-050197-6 (trade
bdg.) — ISBN 978-0-06-050198-3 (lib bdg.)   [1. Saint Patrick's Day—Fiction. 2. Schools—Fiction.]
I. Rockwell, Lizzy, ill. II. Title.   PZ7.R5943Sai 2010   2008020215   [E]—dc22   CIP   AC

Designed by Stephanie Bart-Horvath   10 11 12 13 14 SCP 10 9 8 7 6 5 4 3 2 1   ❖
First Edition

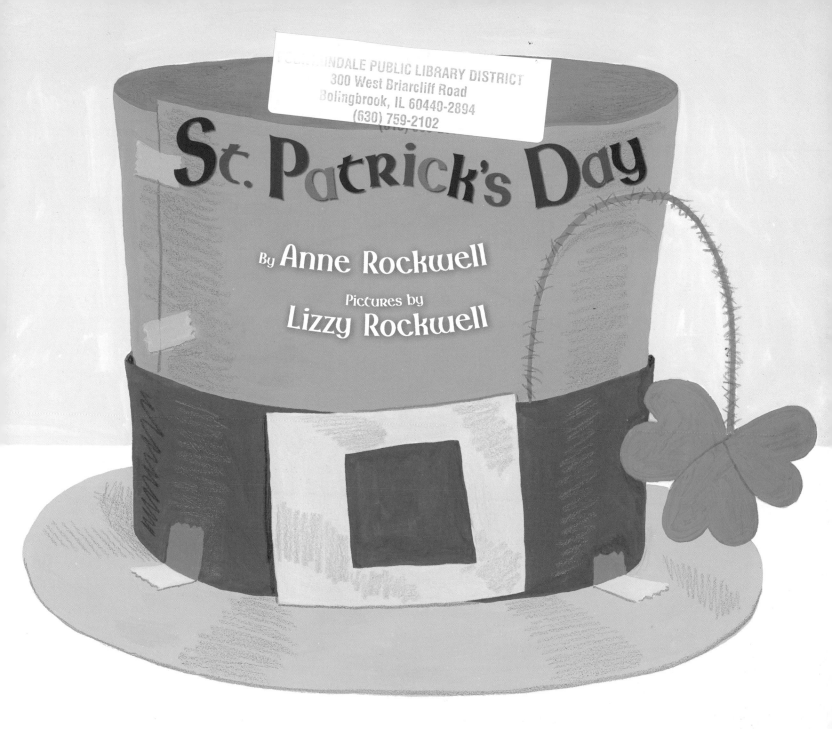

St. Patrick's Day

By Anne Rockwell

Pictures by
Lizzy Rockwell

HARPER

An Imprint of HarperCollinsPublishers

On St. Patrick's Day, I wore my green shirt, green pants, and even my green striped socks. Pablo wore green sneakers.

Everyone wears something green on St. Patrick's Day.
At school, we worked in teams to finish our St. Patrick's Day
reports—Charlie, Jessica, and me; Nicholas and Sarah;
Pablo, Kate, and Sam; and Michiko and Eveline.

Mr. Siscoe helped Charlie and Jessica
and me find out about St. Patrick.
He helped us type the story we told.

This is the story we printed out.

St. Patrick

by Evan and Charlie and Jessica

One bad day, people took St. Patrick from England across the sea to be a slave in Ireland.

Patrick was a shepherd. He didn't fight with anyone. But he missed his mother and father, so he escaped.

But before long he went back to Ireland to teach people to be kind to each other.

Nicholas and Sarah wrote a play.

Nicholas said, "I am St. Patrick.

Do you know why there are no snakes in Ireland?"

"No," everyone replied.

"I drove them away!" said Nicholas.

BOOM, BOOM, BOOM,

CLANG, CLANG, CLANG,

Sarah was a big green snake slithering across the floor.

Nicholas rang his bell and beat his drum.

"Hiss! Hiss! I'm scared!" said Sarah.

"I'm going to run away! Follow me, snakes!"

"Hmm," said Nicholas.

"All the snakes are racing to the sea!

Now you know why there are no snakes in Ireland.

My bell and drum scared them away.

Clang, clang! Boom, boom!"

HISS, HISSsssssss

Pablo, Kate, and Sam love music.
Mr. Kelley, the music teacher, taught
Pablo and Sam how to dance a jig.

Kate fiddled fast
while Sam and Pablo danced.
They wore green top hats.
They looked like the leprechauns that
make mischief on St. Patrick's Day.

Gold

Eveline and Michiko told about the special plant St. Patrick brought to Ireland.

They explained how he planted shamrocks.
Shamrocks are tiny bright green plants
with three round leaves.
They brought a shamrock for each of us in a paper cup.
I'm going to plant mine in our garden.

Mrs. Madoff said so many Irish people came
across the sea to America that we celebrate
St. Patrick's Day whether we're Irish or not.

Many Americans are a little bit Irish,
but not me. I'm all Irish!
My mom and dad were born in Ireland.
My grandparents and my aunts live there.
I went to visit them when I was four.
Here is a picture of me in that green, green land.

When I got home, Mom was baking
soda bread because that's what her mother
always did on St. Patrick's Day.

People put on their best clothes and wore shamrocks.
They went to church to pray the way St. Patrick taught them.
When they came home, they had a fine meal
with soda bread.

We took a loaf to Pablo's mother.
She said it smelled so delicious,
we should have a slice with some hot chocolate.
Yum.

On March 17, we all wear something green.
That's because it's St. Patrick's Day,
and St. Patrick's Day comes just before spring.
The sprouts that come in spring are green.
That day, we are all a little bit Irish.